# I Love My Purse

# I Love My Purse

BY BELLE DeMONT • ART BY SONJA WIMMER

annick press
toronto + berkeley

We acknowledge the support of the Canada Council for the Arts and the Ontario Arts Council, and the participation of the Government of Canada/la participation du gouvernement du Canada for our publishing activities.

| Funded by the Government of Canada | Financé par le gouvernement du Canada |
|---|---|

Cataloging in Publication

DeMont, Belle, author
    I love my purse / Belle DeMont ; Sonja Wimmer, illustrator.

Issued also in electronic formats.
ISBN 978-1-55451-954-5 (hardcover).–ISBN 978-1-55451-955-2 (EPUB).–ISBN 978-1-55451-956-9 (PDF)
    I. Wimmer, Sonja, illustrator  II. Title.
PS8607.E59I46 2017          jC813'.6          C2017-901399-8
                                              C2017-901400-5

Published in the U.S.A. by Annick Press (U.S.) Ltd.
Distributed in Canada by University of Toronto Press.
Distributed in the U.S.A. by Publishers Group West.

Printed in China

www.annickpress.com
www.belledemont.com
www.sonjawimmer.com

Please visit www.annickpress.com/ebooks.html for more details. Or scan

To Olivia and your bright red purse
—B.D.

To my family in Argentina
—S.W.

Every morning, Charlie yawned, stretched, then slid his feet into his favorite fuzzy slippers. And every morning he shuffled over to his closet and looked for something to wear. But there was nothing he liked. Nothing except the bright red purse that his grandma had let him have. So far he had only tried it on in front of the mirror.

One morning Charlie decided enough was enough.

On his way downstairs Charlie passed his dad, who was fumbling with his tie.

"Hold on, wait a second!" said Charlie's dad. "Why are you wearing a purse?"

"'Cause I want to," said Charlie.

"But you're a boy! Boys wear sneakers and baseball caps, not bright red purses!" said his dad.

"But I love my purse!" said Charlie.

"And I love my Hawaiian shirts, but that doesn't mean I can wear them to work! Why don't you wear your backpack instead?"

"Maybe tomorrow, Dad, but today I'm sticking with my purse."

Charlie's dad continued to fumble with his tie, thinking about his Hawaiian shirts.

When Charlie got to school he plopped his purse on the desk, reached in, and pulled out his pencil and eraser.

"Hold on, wait a second," said Charlotte, who sat next to him. "Why are you wearing a purse?"

"'Cause I want to," said Charlie.

"But you're a boy! Boys carry worms in their pockets and toads in their backpacks, not bright red purses!" said Charlotte.

"But I love my purse," said Charlie.

"And I love face paint, but that doesn't mean I should come to school with a different face every day! Why don't you wear a backpack like the rest of the boys?"

"Maybe tomorrow, Charlotte, but today I'm sticking with my purse."

Sophie, who sat behind Charlotte, tapped her on the shoulder. "Ever tried painting a lizard face?"

"A lizard face. That's not a bad idea ..." said Charlotte.

At lunch Charlie nearly walked into a group of older boys.

"Hold on, wait a second," said a boy named Sam. "Why are you wearing a purse?"

"'Cause I want to," said Charlie.

"But you're a boy. Boys ride skateboards and read comic books. We don't wear bright red purses!" Sam said, as his friends laughed.

"But I love my purse," said Charlie.

"And I'd love to eat actual food for lunch every day instead of the stuff they serve us in the cafeteria, but that doesn't mean I can go back in the kitchen and start cooking! Why don't you just wear what the rest of us are wearing?"

"Maybe tomorrow, Sam, but today I'm sticking with my purse."

One of Sam's friends grabbed his shirt. "Come on, or we're gonna end up eating last week's meatloaf."

"See ya, Charlie," said Sam.

On his way home from school, Charlie stopped at the crosswalk.

"Hold on, wait a second," said the crossing guard. "Why are you wearing a purse?"

"'Cause I want to," said Charlie.

"Well I love it!" said the crossing guard. "Have I ever told you about my favorite sparkly shoes?"

The next morning Charlie went downstairs with his purse.

"Still wearing the purse, I see," said Charlie's dad.

"You bet!" said Charlie. "Hold on, where's your tie?"

"I was thinking I'd try something new today," said Charlie's dad.

When Charlie got to school he plopped his purse on his desk.

"Brought the purse again, I see," said Charlotte.

"Sure did," said Charlie. "Hold on, what's all over your face?"

"Oh, whoops! That must be paint. I was practicing my snow queen this morning."

At lunchtime, Sam walked up to Charlie in the cafeteria.

"Still wearing the purse, I see," said Sam.

"Yep," said Charlie, looking at the lunch menu.
"Ugh, tuna casserole for the third day in a row!"

"Not for me. I brought my homemade spaghetti
Bolognese," said Sam, showing Charlie his lunch.
Charlie's stomach growled.

Charlie wore his purse every day that week. On Friday he went downstairs for breakfast and found his dad flipping flapjacks in the kitchen. He was wearing his favorite Hawaiian shirt.

"Hold on, wait a second. Why aren't you wearing your suit, Dad?" asked Charlie.

"I love this shirt. The world needs to see it!" proclaimed his dad.

"You don't think your boss is gonna get mad?" asked Charlie.

"Only thing he could get mad about is not owning this sweet shirt!" said Charlie's dad.

When Charlie got to school he plopped his purse on his desk.

"Hold on, wait a second. You're wearing face paint!" Charlie said to Charlotte, who had painted herself to look (sort of) like a tiger.

"I love trying out different faces. The world needs
to see these skills!" said Charlotte proudly.

At lunch time the most delicious aroma filled the cafeteria.

"What's for lunch today?" Charlie asked the lunch lady, just as Sam popped out of the kitchen. He was wearing a chef's hat and stirring something in a giant silver bowl.

"Charlie! I'm so glad you're here! I just finished the risotto. You're gonna love it," said Sam.

"Hold on, wait a second. What are you doing in the kitchen?" asked Charlie.

"I love to cook good food. And I know we were all getting tired of the stuff they were serving us."

"HEY!" said the lunch ladies.

When Charlie got to the crosswalk on his way home, he saw that the crossing guard was wearing a very sparkly pair of shoes.

"Hold on, wait a second—I love your shoes!" said Charlie.

"It's about time I wore them!"
said the crossing guard.

"You know, those shoes remind
me of something I forgot I had
in the back of my closet ..."
said Charlie.